Published by
North Atlantic Books
Huichin, unceded Ohlone land
aka Berkeley, California

Printed in Canada

Cover art and design by Megan Herbert
Book design by Happenstance Type-O-Rama

The Tantrum That Saved the World is sponsored and published by North Atlantic Books, an educational nonprofit based in the unceded Ohlone land Huichin (aka Berkeley, CA), that collaborates with partners to develop cross-cultural perspectives, nurture holistic views of art, science, the humanities, and healing, and seed personal and global transformation by publishing work on the relationship of body, spirit, and nature.

North Atlantic Books' publications are distributed to the US trade and internationally by Penguin Random House Publishers Services. For further information, visit our website at www.northatlanticbooks.com.

Library of Congress Cataloging-in-Publication Data

Names: Herbert, Megan, 1977—author | Mann, Michael E., author.
Title: The Tantrum That Saved the World / Megan Herbert.
Description: Berkeley, California : North Atlantic Books, 2022. | Audience: Ages 5-9. | Audience: Grades 2-3. | Summary: Approached by a variety of people and animals driven out of their homes by climate change, a young girl heads to the halls of power and throws a tantrum that just might save the world. Includes a science section explaining global warming, climate change, and the perils of environmental destruction.
Identifiers: LCCN 2021015021 (print) | LCCN 2021015022 (ebook) | ISBN 9781623176846 (hardcover) | ISBN 9781623176853 (epub)
Subjects: LCSH: Climatic changes—Juvenile fiction. | Environmental degradation—Juvenile fiction. | Environmental responsibility—Juvenile fiction. | Compassion—Juvenile fiction. | Stories in rhyme. | Picture books for children. | CYAC: Stories in rhyme. | Climatic changes—Fiction. | Environmental degradation—Fiction. | LCGFT: Stories in rhyme. | Picture books.
Classification: LCC PZ8.3 .H4199 Tan 2022 (print) | LCC PZ8.3 (ebook) | DDC 813.6 [E]—dc23
LC record available at https://lccn.loc.gov/2021015021
LC ebook record available at https://lccn.loc.gov/2021015022

1 2 3 4 5 6 7 8 9 Friesens 28 27 26 25 24 23 22

This book includes recycled material and material from well-managed forests. North Atlantic Books is committed to the protection of our environment. We print on recycled paper whenever possible and partner with printers who strive to use environmentally responsible practices.

The TANTRUM That SAVED the WORLD

For my son, Maksim, to whom I want to leave a healthy world.
And for Sruli, who makes me brave.
—M.H.

To my daughter, Megan Mann, whose generation
will inherit the earth we leave behind.
—M.E.M.

The TANTRUM That SAVED the WORLD

BY MEGAN HERBERT
and
MICHAEL E. MANN

North Atlantic Books

Huichin, unceded Ohlone land
aka Berkeley, California

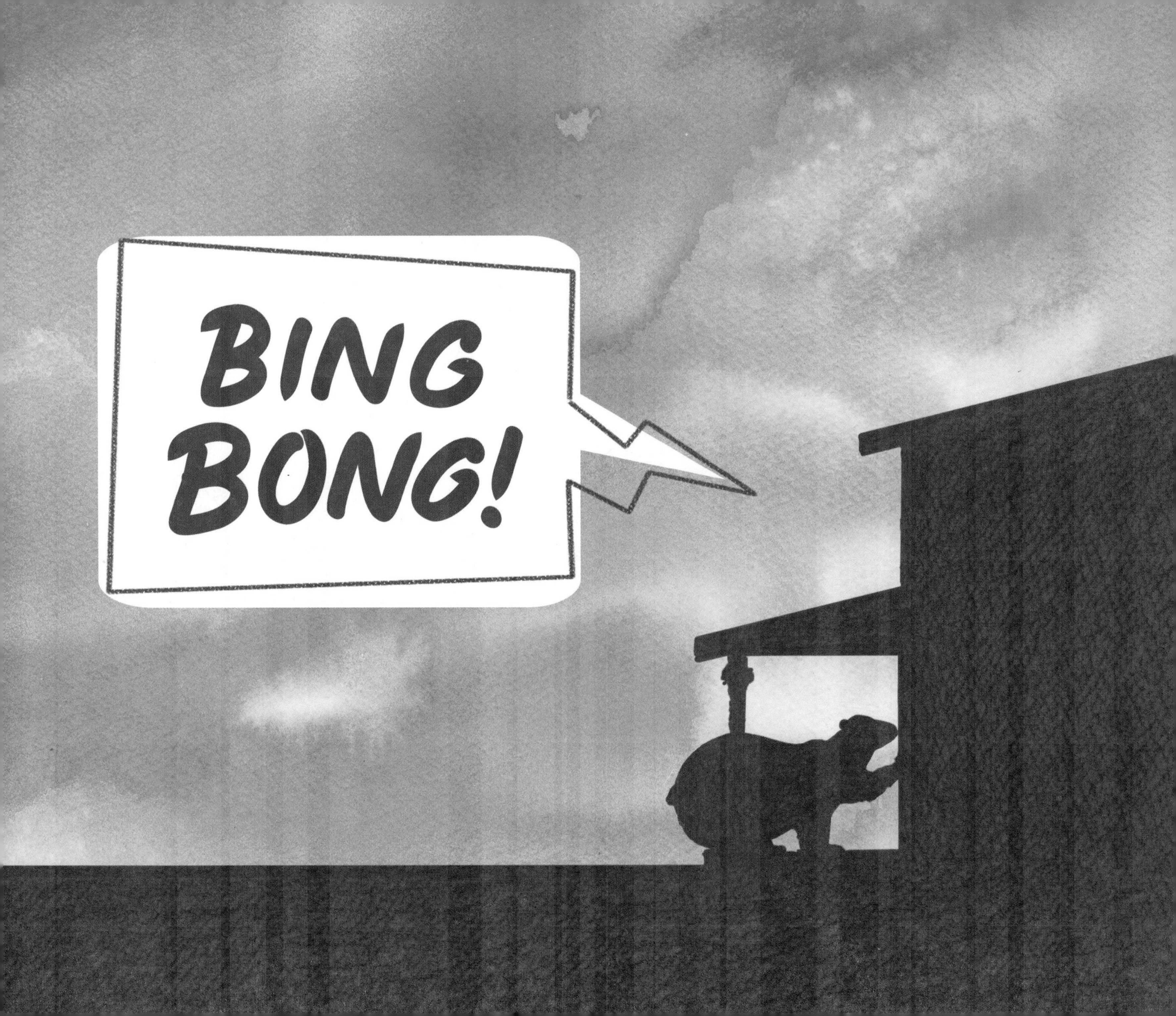
BING
BONG!

Sophia was minding her business one day,

When, quite without warning, a bear came to stay.

The ice that he lived on had ceased to exist.

He hoped that Sophia would kindly assist.

Startled and flustered, Sophia said, **"No."**

But the bear came right in. He had nowhere to go.

More out-of-towners arrived needing aid,
Asking if it was all right that they stayed.
"Somehow the seas have flooded our land."

The kids ran right in.
They were quite out of hand.

Sophia attempted to turn them away.

"We've got nowhere else," was all they could say.

Surprising arrivals showed up all day long.

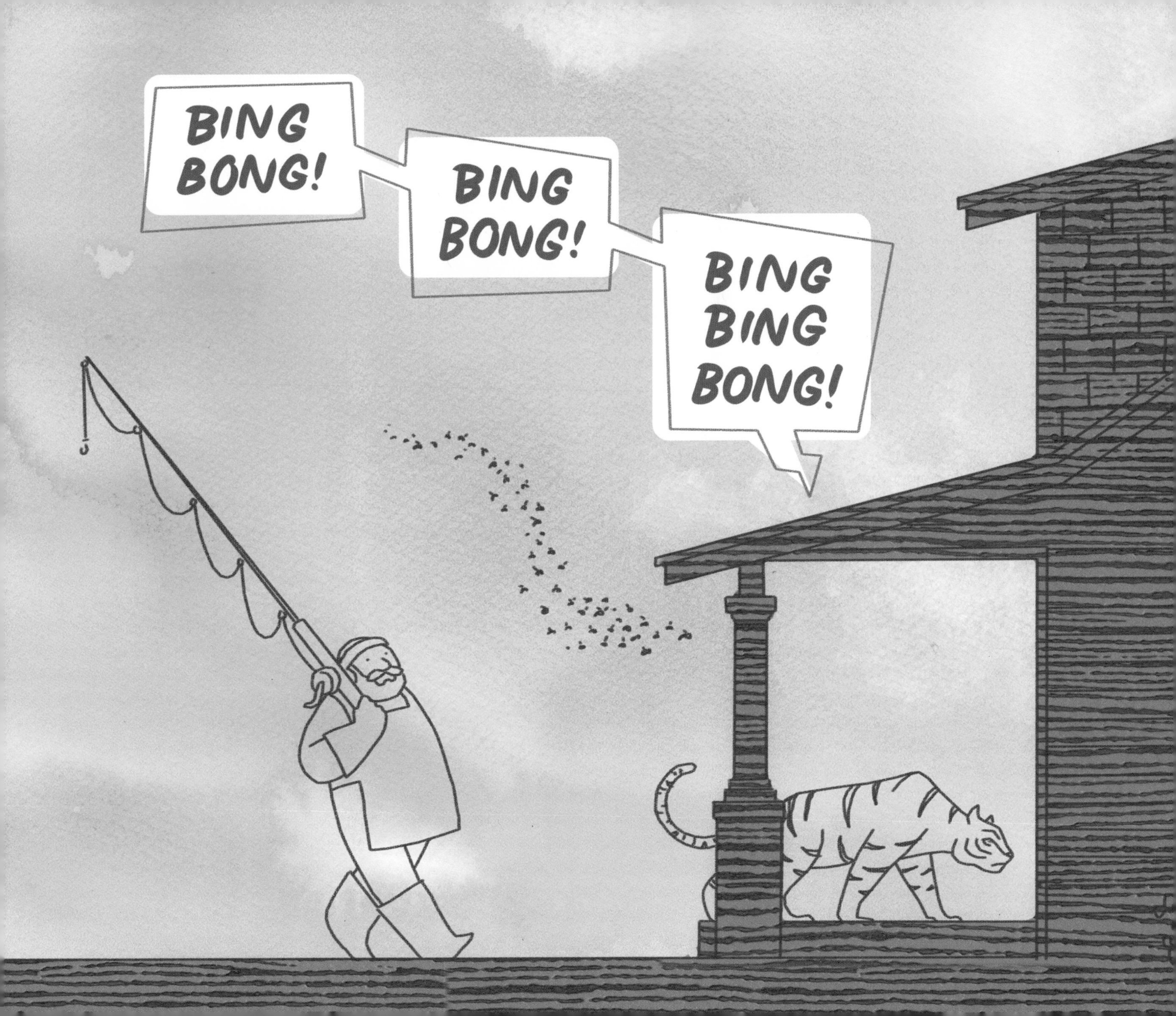
BING BONG!
BING BONG!
BING BING BONG!

A sad swarm of bees had not one idea, if spring had just come or fall was quite near.

A pale pink flamingo, hungry and weak, bugged a sea turtle whose outlook was bleak.

Both were upset that the sites of their nests

Were being disrupted by unwanted guests.

Farmers whose farmland was withered and dry

Griped with the seaman who couldn't get by.

Where had the fish gone? Where was the rain?

They wanted to work more, not sit and complain.

A large Bengal tiger just chuffed with dismay.

Everyone wisely stayed out of his way.

They all turned to face her with hope in their eyes, expecting Sophia to halt their demise.

Sophia, by this time, felt nothing but stress.

Her day was disrupted. Her house was a mess.

She had no idea how she ought to begin,

To help them all out of the bind they were in.

Unable to put up a front anymore,

She went to her bedroom and slammed shut the door.

Hiding and fretting, she couldn't think why,

These folks were resolved to gray up her blue sky.

She wanted to scream, and to act uncontrolled.

But tantrums were pointless, that's what she'd been told.

Still . . .

It wasn't Sophia's fault they were in strife!

She'd tell them, politely, to get out of her life.

But what she saw next brought Sophia up short.

They weren't here to spite her.

They needed support!

All of a sudden, the girl understood:

Good will costs nothing, and does nothing but good.

Now that she'd realized compassion was key,

Sophia would call on the powers that be.

"Let's go!" said Sophia. "Next stop City Hall."

The grown-ups would sort this mess once and for all.

"I need an appointment regarding this fauna,
Who've noticed our planet's becoming a sauna.
So, bring us the top dog, the biggest big cheese,
To solve all our problems and put us at ease."

They said, "Take a number and wait, if you please."

Sophia attempted to move things along.

"The fact we've been waiting so long is quite wrong . . .

. . . this tiger's hungrier by the minute.

. . . this pink flamingo's reached her limit.

. . . this polar bear is far too warm.

. . . these bees can hardly form a swarm."

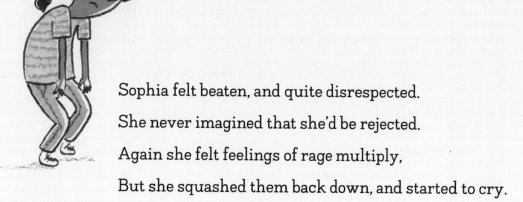

Sophia felt beaten, and quite disrespected.

She never imagined that she'd be rejected.

Again she felt feelings of rage multiply,

But she squashed them back down, and started to cry.

Her friends, also glum, gathered round in support,

They all shared their stories to make the wait short.

Sophia soon saw how each tale was connected,

That *everyone* loses when one part's neglected.

How would she feel if her land were depleted?

Her food disappeared? Her home overheated?

And what was to say that she wouldn't be next?

She'd already noticed weird weather effects.

How could their leaders command them to wait?

If they dilly-dallied, would it be too late?

Sophia thought deeply and then made her choice ...

She had to give those who'd been silenced a voice.

Pushed to the limit, Sophia saw RED.

She felt disregarded and mocked and misled.

She did understand what this was about.

It was her future they planned to sell out.

Sophia's strong feelings smoldered once more,

And this time they'd gotten too big to ignore.

Raging with purpose, her banner unfurled,

She kicked off a tantrum to *SAVE THE WHOLE WORLD!*

It rumbled down streets, into towns of all lands.

It echoed in forests, on glaciers and sands.

People and creatures alike felt its force.

They ditched their distractions and looked for the source.

There were Sophia and friends holding court,

Telling the people to lend their support.

Cooperative action could turn this high tide.

They had strength in numbers and right on their side.

Step one was to stop using oil, gas, and coal.

Step two was to educate every last soul,

On practical things they could do every day,

To have an effect in a positive way.

They told their officials inside City Hall

To pass laws with foresight to better them all.

They all told more people, who told more folks still.

They won hearts with kindness and minds with good will.

And so on and so on until everyone

Was doing the hard work that had to be done.

Sophia's new friends soon waved her goodbye.

They'd made second chances, had new homes to try.

They asked her to visit, for a weekend or two...

But Sophia was busy.

She had things to do.

WHAT ARE GLOBAL WARMING AND CLIMATE CHANGE?

For hundreds of years humans have used *fossil fuels* to make the energy that warms and lights homes, and powers transportation and industry. Over time, scientists noticed that burning these *fossil fuels* made *carbon dioxide*, a *greenhouse gas*, build up in Earth's atmosphere. When *greenhouse gases* build up, they act like a blanket, warming up the lower part of Earth's atmosphere. This process, called *global warming*, can melt glacial ice, causing *sea level rise*, moving rainfall patterns, and increasing *extreme weather events*. The changes happening in nature from this warming are known as *climate change*.

Climate change is disrupting the Earth's *ecosystems*, and threatening the plants, people, and animals that live there. Those who have to leave their homes because of *climate change* are sometimes called *climate refugees*.

If we act quickly, we can stop the changes happening to our climate. First, we should use only *renewable energy sources* that do not make *greenhouse gases*. Second, we must live in harmony with the natural world; how we travel, feed ourselves, make things, and use and dispose of things should create as small a *carbon footprint* as possible to stop more *greenhouse gases* from building up.

The following pages explain the stories of the *climate refugees* Sophia meets, how *climate change* is affecting their homes and *habitats*, and what can be done to help them.

Words written in *italics* are further explained in the Glossary.

MELTING ICE

Global warming is heating up Earth's *polar regions* even faster than the rest of the planet, causing the ice there to melt. The meltwater flows into the ocean and causes *sea level rise*.

In the Arctic, which is mostly ocean, the ice exists as a thin layer floating on the sea, called sea ice. Polar bears float on the sea ice when they hunt seals, their main food source. When the sea ice melts, the polar bears cannot hunt for seals, and they go hungry.

What's more, as the ice melts, the oceans absorb more sunlight, causing them to warm even faster, melting even more ice.

The good news is that we can adapt to small shifts in climate and moderate *sea level rise* if we move quickly to reduce our use of *fossil fuels*.

SEA LEVEL RISE

Far away from where the ice is melting, *sea level rise* is causing *coastal erosion* and flooding. Low-lying island nations are especially vulnerable to these *climate change* effects. Kiribati, a group of *coral atolls* in the Pacific Ocean, is one such place. New corals grow a calcium carbonate, or limestone, skeleton. This ring of limestone, or reef, usually acts as a barrier from the surrounding ocean. But sea levels are rising faster than the reef can build up, and *ocean acidification* is damaging the growth of the coral. As the islands' coasts are eroded by waves, saltwater moves inland, polluting the soil and the freshwater supplies. That makes growing enough food to feed the people living there difficult. The I-Kiribati will likely be forced to leave the islands in the near future making them *climate refugees*.

Even large cities, like America's New York, Japan's Osaka, and Rotterdam in the Netherlands, are at risk from coastal flooding. Some of these places already have flood protection systems in place. But prevention is a better idea. By stopping activities that create CO_2 emissions, we can prevent coastal flooding and find ways to live together on a planet with limited resources and a growing population.

POLLINATION

Bee and other insect populations are declining around the world. The reasons for this include *habitat loss*, the use of pesticides (chemical sprays) in farming, and *climate change*, which is disturbing the relationships between plants and animals.

Bees are *pollinators*. They collect nectar, a sweet and nutritious food source, from inside flowers. In return, bees pollinate the flowers, moving pollen from one flower to the next. This process fertilizes plants so they can grow seeds and fruit. Bees and plants working together in this way is called symbiosis, meaning they depend on each other to survive, and their life cycles happen at the same time. *Climate change* is affecting the natural cycle of the seasons, causing the spring warm-up to happen earlier each year. When bees mature and plants flower at different times, their symbiotic relationship goes out of rhythm. That is a problem not only for the plants and *pollinators,* but also for people, who depend on the food that comes from those plants. Coffee, apples, oranges, and honey are just some of the foods that result from *pollination*.

Slowing down *global warming* will give *pollinators* and plants time to adapt to the changes that are happening.

THE ANIMAL FOOD CHAIN AND MIGRATION

Andean flamingos living in the wetlands of the Andes of South America are threatened by *climate change*. As the glaciers of the Andean mountains shrink, the wetlands are robbed of meltwater, and local mining and farming is polluting and depleting the water that remains. As their *habitat* is disrupted, so too is their *food chain*. The flamingos' pink color comes from the brine shrimp they eat. Just like the *crustaceans* who are food for seals, who in turn are food for polar bears, these tiny shrimp are affected by *ocean acidification*. Flamingos are generally nonmigratory, which means that they stay in one place. But with their *habitats* and food sources endangered, they too risk becoming *climate refugees*.

As the earth heats up, both terrestrial (land-based) and marine (water-based) animals are migrating toward cooler climates. Disease-carrying insects, like mosquitoes and ticks, are spreading disease farther. Bark beetles living in Northern Hemisphere forests are moving closer to *polar regions*, attacking trees already weakened by longer, hotter summers, increasing the risk of forest fires, which in turn release more planet-warming CO_2.

Preventing the buildup of CO_2 in our atmosphere and oceans will limit further migration and give all animal and plant species time to adapt.

THE IMPORTANCE OF HEALTHY OCEANS

The ocean is the world's biggest, most diverse *ecosystem*. It provides half of our oxygen, absorbs heat and *carbon dioxide*, and provides vital food sources. When oceans are at risk, so is all life on Earth.

As ocean waters warm up, coral reefs, a key *habitat* for sea turtles, are impacted. *Ocean acidification* dissolves not only the skeletons of the corals but also the shells of *crustaceans* and other shell-forming creatures living there, which are an important part of the *food chain* for larger sea creatures. Warming oceans also result in more female than male turtle hatchlings being born. With fewer males to mate with the females, fewer turtles are born with each generation. Add to this the problem of *coastal erosion*, which makes it difficult for turtles to return from the ocean to the beaches where they were hatched to have babies of their own.

Scientists predict that oceans will return to full health if we combat *climate change*, stop overfishing, and protect the ocean to give it time to recover from the damage done. This would benefit not only marine life, but humans as well, who rely on the health of the oceans to survive.

RISING TEMPERATURES AND DROUGHTS

Agricultural (or food-growing) regions around the world are already seeing the effects of *climate change*. In North African countries, including Egypt, Algeria, and Sudan, daytime temperatures can reach 115°F (46°C), with nighttime temperatures never cooling below 86°F (30°C). Such conditions are simply too hot for humans to live comfortably.

Meanwhile, droughts in *subtropical regions* are destroying farms and creating conditions that make wildfires more likely.

The ongoing Syrian drought, which began at the start of the twenty-first century, and was almost certainly worsened by *climate change*, is the worst the region has seen in at least 900 years. The drought has ruined Syrian farms, forcing more than a million Syrian farmers and their families to move into the cities. When more people have to live in cramped conditions sharing the limited water and food supplies, local disagreements often arise, as they have in Syria, causing Syrians to escape to other parts of the world for safety.

In our interconnected world, working together is the key to solving problems that will affect us all.

JOBS AND INFRASTRUCTURE

The cold New England waters were a good breeding ground for marine species because cold water can hold more oxygen. Just like us, marine animals need oxygen to live. As waters warm, seafood species like swordfish, cod, and lobster have to move farther north to cooler waters to survive.

Disturbance to one part of an *ecosystem* or *food chain* can affect the entire community, including the fishermen whose jobs depend on the health of seafood populations, and people who eat seafood as a source of protein. It is important to balance the needs of these people with carefully managed fishing practices, so that ocean species can survive.

It isn't just jobs that are at risk. *Extreme weather events* can damage *infrastructure* and disrupt delivery of food and other goods. Convincing governments and businesses to use *renewable energy sources* now will lessen the damage done by *climate change* and create new jobs in industries that work in harmony with Earth's living systems.

DEFORESTATION AND HABITAT LOSS

The survival of the Bengal tiger is threatened by poaching (illegal hunting), *deforestation*, and *habitat* loss. The Sundarbans, which is a series of mangrove forests in Bangladesh and India that lie at the mouth of the great Ganges River, are home to hundreds of species of fish, *reptiles*, *mammals*, and birds, as well as the small number of remaining wild Bengal tigers on Earth. The roots of mangrove trees join together in a network, forming a unique forested environment in the shallow tidal zone at the ocean's edge. Mangrove forests provide shelter and food for marine life and protect the coastal wetlands from extreme weather. With just one foot of *sea level rise*, most of the Sundarbans would be covered by the ocean, taking the home of the Bengal tiger with it.

To protect this *habitat* and the creatures who live there, we can tell governments to do more to conserve mangrove swamps, and to stop poachers. Slowing down *global warming* and *sea level rise* might also allow time for the mangrove forests to migrate inland slowly.

GLOSSARY

Carbon dioxide, or CO$_2$: Carbon dioxide is a greenhouse gas produced naturally when plants and animals breathe. The burning of fossil fuels can also create CO$_2$. Too much of it in our atmosphere causes warming of the planet and climate change.

Carbon footprint: The amount of CO$_2$ emissions created by a person, company, action, or event.

Climate change: The human-caused warming of the planet, and the changes in wind and air currents, rainfall patterns, weather events, and sea levels that come with it.

Climate refugees: People (and, in our story, animals) who must leave their homes or homelands, due to the effects of climate change.

Coastal erosion: The loss of land along a coastline due to waves, weather, and rising tides.

Coral atolls: Ring-shaped islands that are formed on top of coral reefs left behind when a volcanic island slowly sinks beneath the sea.

Crustaceans: Animals with a hard exoskeleton (outer shell) who have limbs and eyes, but no internal skeleton. Almost all of them live in water.

Deforestation: The cutting down or burning of forests to clear land for industry. This adds to rising greenhouse gas levels by leaving fewer trees to absorb CO$_2$, and releasing more CO$_2$ when the wood is burned.

Ecosystem: All living things (like plants, animals, and other organisms) and nonliving things (like soil, climate, and water) in an area. There are terrestrial (land) ecosystems and aquatic (water) ecosystems, with many different categories in each.

Extreme weather events: Floods, heat waves, droughts, and powerful storms. Climate change can increase their number and strength in many regions of the world.

Food chain: The order in which living things depend on each other for food. Every ecosystem has one or more food chains that overlap and connect.

Fossil fuels: Oil, gasoline, natural gas, and coal. Coal comes from organic matter (plants and animals), long ago buried beneath Earth's surface, transforming over time. When these materials are burned to generate energy, they release CO_2 into Earth's atmosphere.

Global warming: The warming of Earth's surface and lower atmosphere due to an increase in greenhouse gas concentrations.

Greenhouse gas: Gases, such as carbon dioxide and methane, that absorb and trap some of the heat escaping from Earth's surface out to space, warming the earth and its atmosphere.

Habitat: A place where a plant or animal normally makes its home in nature.

Infrastructure: Cities and towns, buildings, roads, transportation systems, bridges, dams, and other human-made structures or institutions that make up the human-built environment.

Mammals: Warm-blooded vertebrates (with a backbone) who breathe air and typically grow hair or fur. Female mammals produce milk to feed their young.

Ocean acidification: As more carbon dioxide builds up in the atmosphere and enters the ocean, the ocean waters become more acidic.

Polar region: The regions of Earth near the South and North Poles, which receive fewer of the sun's warming rays, and tend to be cold and covered by ice or snow.

Pollinators and pollination: Pollination happens when pollinators (insects, birds, and bats) move pollen between flowering plants, allowing fruits, seeds, and baby plants to grow.

Renewable energy sources: Sources of energy such as wind, solar, hydrothermal, and geothermal that do not generate carbon pollution and will never run out.

Reptiles: Cold-blooded, scaly vertebrates (with a backbone) who breathe air and lay eggs. While some reptiles live completely or partly in the water, nearly all lay their eggs on land.

Sea level rise: The rise in sea levels caused by the melting of glaciers and ice sheets and the expansion of ocean water as it warms.

Subtropical regions: Dry, warm, regions of Earth: the southwestern United States, the Sahara and sub-Saharan Africa, the Middle East, South Africa, and much of Australia.

 Scan to download and print the "World Saving Action Plan" poster included as a foldout in this book.

SOPHIA HEREBY THANKS THE FOLLOWING
WORLD SAVING HEROES

Virginia and John Allen

Samuel Jirra Birchall

Hillary Clinton

Kim Cobb

Finn Hendrix Colbert

Dadso

Hamilton de Moyer

Peyton de Moyer

Eurocorrespondent (Belgium) SPRL

Harrison Fichtner

Ronan Hadj-Chikh

Charles Henry

Sally Herbert

Jennifer R. Holmgren

Gabriel Lamb

LanzaTech

Sienna and Aidan Lightman

Megan Mann

Lisa Marianne

Alice Naoumova

Arwen, Rhana, and Elara Nicholson

Charlotte and Henry Oliver

Maksim Valentin Recht

Lillian Madison Schneider

Ruth Scolnik

Lily Stevens

Dashiell Haxby Summit

Joseph Wick

Rose Wick

*And all the people who pledged
their support to help bring this book into being.*

ABOUT THE AUTHORS

MEGAN HERBERT is an Australian-born writer, illustrator, and cartoonist. Her first edition of *The Tantrum That Saved The World* was awarded a 2018 Moonbeam Award for books about Environmental Issues and the 2019 American Meteorological Society's Louis J. Battan Award for Best Children's Book, K-12.

MICHAEL E. MANN is Distinguished Professor of Atmospheric Science at Penn State, with joint appointments in the Department of Geosciences and the Earth and Environmental Systems Institute (EESI). He is also director of the Penn State Earth System Science Center (ESSC). Dr. Mann has received numerous awards and contributed, with other IPCC authors, to the award of the 2007 Nobel Peace Prize. You can view his full bio at https://michaelmann.net.